לד' הארץ ומלואה

This book belongs to:

Kaila KVETCHES No More

M. Jakubowicz

Illustrated by
Yocheved Nadell

ISBN 978-1-60091-612-0

Published by:
Israel Bookshop Publications
501 Prospect Street
Lakewood, NJ 08701
Tel: (732) 901-3009 / Fax: (732) 901-4012
www.israelbookshoppublications.com
info@israelbookshoppublications.com

Printed in Bulgaria

Distributed in Israel by:
Tfutza Publications
P.O.B. 50036
Beitar Illit 90500
972-2-650-9400

Distributed in Europe by:
Lehmanns
Unit E Viking Industrial Park
Rolling Mill Road
Jarrow, Tyne & Wear NE32 3DP
44-191-430-0333

Distributed in Australia by:
Gold's Book and Gift Company
3-13 William Street
Balaclava 3183
613-9527-8775

Distributed in South Africa by:
Kollel Bookshop
Northfield Centre
17 Northfield Avenue
Glenhazel 2192
27-11-440-6679

To all the kids out there
Who try hard to watch the
way they speak
And view the world around
them with an *ayin tovah*

This story is for you!

This is the story of Kaila,
Who complained all night and day.
No matter what was going on,
She had nothing nice to say!

The weather was too hot or cold;
The sky too dim or bright.
Her hair was too short or too long;
Her shoes too loose or tight.

Her Shabbos clothes were plain,
And her house was way too small.
Her brother was too noisy;
She could hear him through the wall!

SALE

School was way too boring;
Camp just wasn't fun.
The pool was much too shady,
While the yard was in the sun.

Car rides made her sick,
While walking was a bore.
She didn't like to shop
Because of long lines at the store.

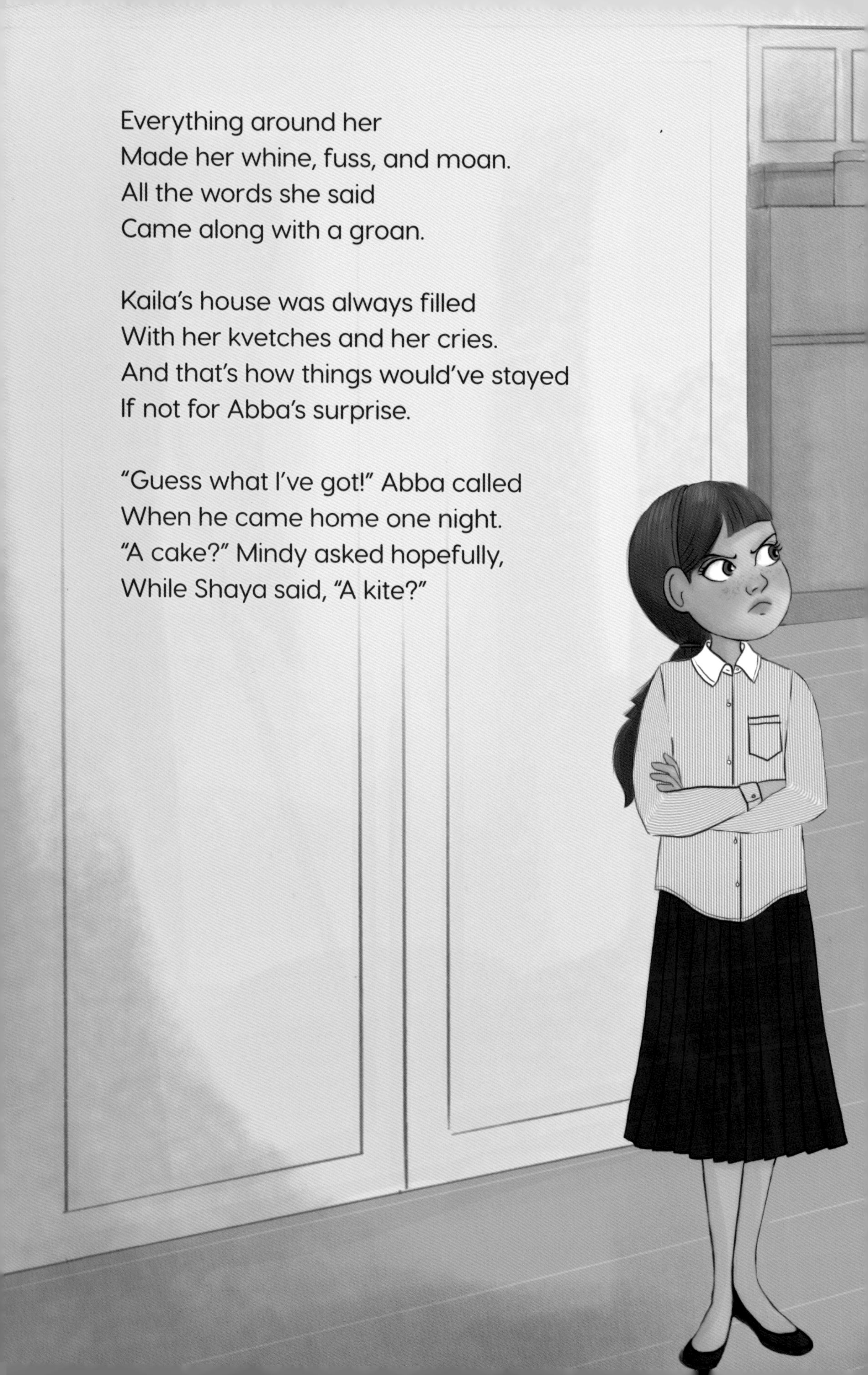

Everything around her
Made her whine, fuss, and moan.
All the words she said
Came along with a groan.

Kaila's house was always filled
With her kvetches and her cries.
And that's how things would've stayed
If not for Abba's surprise.

"Guess what I've got!" Abba called
When he came home one night.
"A cake?" Mindy asked hopefully,
While Shaya said, "A kite?"

"Nope," Abba said with a grin,
And he lifted a large, red sheet.
There was a cage with a big, bright bird.
"Here's a pet for you to meet!"

"A parrot!" said Kaila loudly,
And she stared hard at the bird.
"It's not as nice as others I've seen."
The parrot echoed every word!

"Let's call our new bird Tuki,"
Shaya said with pride.
"I don't like that name," Kaila claimed,
But–"Tuki!" the parrot cried.

Kaila kvetched and cried
While Mommy served peas and fish.
She whined out loud as always,
Complained about every dish.

Tuki squawked and squealed,
"I don't like! I don't like!"
Abba chuckled and said,
"That bird has its own mike!"

"It's really way too loud!"
Kaila said and then sighed.
"It's really way too loud!"
Tuki shouted and cried.

Kaila covered her ears
And glared at the bird's sharp beak.
Did Tuki care? Not a bit!
"Don't like!" he continued to shriek.

Kaila awoke the next morning
To a day that was cold and wet.
With the sky so gray and gloomy,
How could she not be upset?

Her favorite shirt was dirty;
Her skirt wasn't pleated right.
Things were going from bad to worse
When she suddenly had a fright!

"Hey!" she yelled at Shaya.
"You scared me when you threw
That ball in my direction!
What is *wrong* with you?"

"What's wrong with you?" Tuki screeched
Right into Kaila's ear.
"Oh, no!" she cried. "I woke that bird!
I forgot that he was here!"

Kaila closed the door and cried,
"I'm going to be so late!
Do I have to go to school?
It's already almost eight!"

She shouted and ranted and raved,
And complained and whined some more...
That's when she heard "Be so late!"
Coming right through the closed door.

It was Tuki, if you haven't guessed,
Repeating her every word.
What else would you come to expect
From this friendly, colored bird?

Kaila covered her ears
And decided to leave right away.
"I don't want to stay and listen
To this bird copy me all day!"

But school didn't go too well–
Kaila's snack was stale and hard;
Her project came out crooked;
It was too wet to play in the yard.

So who could blame poor Kaila
When she came stomping home that day?
“How was school?” her mother asked.
“It was bad in every way!”

"Bad in every way!"
Tuki screeched with all his might.
Kaila jumped out of her seat,
As she looked around in fright.

"I forgot about that bird,"
She said, shaking her head.
"Can't we get rid of it *now*,
And get a quiet pet instead?"

"Don't you see, my dearest Kaila?"
Mommy said as she stirred a pot.
"Tuki repeats the words you shout,
Whether you like it or not!

"There's nothing wrong with Tuki–
He just copies the words you speak.
It's up to you if he'll say nice things
Or if he will screech and shriek."

That night when supper was served,
It was one of Kaila's worst.
Still, she said not one word,
Though she thought that she would burst!

"How was your day?" Abba asked,
When Kaila had finished her rice.
Kaila thought a bit and then said,
"My day was kind of...nice."

"My day was kind of nice!"
Tuki cawed, cackled, and cooed.
As Kaila listened to Tuki,
She was in a better mood!

The next morning Kaila found
That someone had taken her snack!
Guess who woke up from her shouts?
"My snack!" Tuki screamed back.

So Kaila swallowed hard
And bit back her next word.
She'd gotten her reminder
In the form of her pet bird.

Kaila kept on thinking,
What will my new bird say?
It made her look for the good–
And she had a pretty great day!

Kaila has slowly changed,
With Tuki at her side.
She's learned to speak calmly
And how to smile wide.

But the best thing that happened
Took place in Kaila's head,
Because acting in this way
Caused her happiness to spread.

At last she began to see
That life *is* truly great.
Now when she looks around,
There's so much to appreciate!

And if she forgets and complains,
Tuki is right there to shriek—
Then Kaila quickly remembers
The correct way to think and speak!